MW01713536

Beware the Hawk

A.J. O'Connell

Vagabondage Press

Beware the Hawk

ISBN-13: 978-0615611037
ISBN-10: 0615611036

Vagabondage Press
PO Box 3563
Apollo Beach, Florida 33572
http://www.vagabondagepress.com

First print edition released in the United States of America and the United Kingdom, March 2012

10 9 8 7 6 5 4 3 2

Cover photo by Roberto A Sanchez. Cover designed by N. Apythia Morges.

Beware the Hawk

For Pencils, my first writing group.

Beware the Hawk

I hurt my ankle almost as soon as I stepped into Boston.

There is this certain kind of slime that you can find in the gutters of Chinatown. I don't know what it's made of, but as soon as you cross over the invisible line that separates Chinatown from the Financial District, it's all over the place. You can't smell it in the winter, but it's there, congealed into pools of greasy ice. I put my foot through the Chinatown gate, right onto a sheet of the stuff and went down. My left leg went out in front of me, and the rest of me came down on my right. It was 3 a.m. No one was around to offer me a hand up. A few taxis cruised by, getting onto the Mass Pike. No cops. No passersby. No bums even. It was that cold. I grabbed my ankle and howled.

My pocket buzzed. I blinked away the little balls of white light that were exploding in my field of vision and, breathing hard, looked down at my iPhone. I had three missed text messages from Leo:

R SAYS TO MEET YOU TONIGHT, MY SWEET

AM AT SNOW FLOWER

IT'S 2:30 AM. WHERE THE FUCK ARE YOU?

"Fuck you, Leo," I whispered and poked my ankle to see if it was broken. It wasn't my idea to be here. I had orders.

I'd just come in from New York on the rolling third-world country that is the Fung-Wah bus. That wasn't my idea either; I'd slipped into bed in Brooklyn at 10 p.m., looking forward to a good, long night of sleep, but as soon as I'd flipped off the light, my iPhone lit up, and I heard the special ring, the one I should never, ever ignore. I swore and picked it up.

"The Resistance needs you in Boston tonight." The voice at the other end of the line was gravelly. I didn't recognize it.

"The Resistance should have told me sooner." Normally I didn't bitch to the boss, but it was late; I was cranky. "I'll never get there tonight. Not even if you guys put me on a plane."

"A Fung-Wah leaves Chinatown in an hour. It's the last one tonight. Be on it."

"An hour? I'll have to take a taxi." I was already pulling off my pajama bottoms.

"You ought to be able to afford it. We pay you enough. Contact Leo in Boston."

"Oh Jesus." I pulled my messenger bag off the closet door and began tossing in extra pairs of underwear and socks. "I hate Leo."

"Do it," said the voice. "You're picking something up this time. Leo will know more about it."

I was at the Fung-Wah terminal by 10:45. I always did everything that the Resistance told me to do.

I limped down the sidewalk. Chinatown was dead at 3 a.m. on any morning. There was only one unshuttered door in the whole neighborhood, and that was the one I wanted. Boston has this law that all places that sell alcohol have to close by two. So at two, this place turned down the music and pretended to stop selling alcohol. Alcohol wasn't its major trade anyhow.

I pushed through the door and fished out the necessary ID. The bouncer's eyebrow rose when he took in my highlighter-pink hair and Hello Kitty wallet, but eyed the card and passed it back to me. He wasn't checking my date of birth, anyhow.

"You're here for Leo," he said. I nodded.

He jerked a thumb over his shoulder. "He's here."

It was quiet in that bar, and dark. You could barely see the walls. One wizened old man sat at the bar. A few people sat in booths. Some guy from the Financial District murmured with an aging prostitute, negotiating out of the cold. Another guy sat with his head propped against the wall. A faint haze hung near the ceiling. All the regulars were upstairs. I hoped that Leo wasn't up there too, because I hated the drooling and the clutching hands; I hated the stink of it. You may think that opium dens are a thing of the past, like something operated by nefarious Chinese men in Rudyard Kipling novels, but the industry is alive and well. You just need to know where to look, if you're into that sort of thing, which I'm not.

Leo, on the other hand, is. He's into a lot of shit. He'd drink absinthe — I'm talking about the good, Victorian-style stuff — like Lemon Fanta, if he could get his hands on enough of it. I was hoping that he abstained for the evening. If he was in the den upstairs, it'd be a long wait before he would be useful to me. I knew that from experience.

I limped all the way to the back of the room, scanning the tables for the familiar oily hair and leather jacket. Amazingly enough, there in the corner booth where he said he'd be, was Leo.

Leo always had a vaguely homeless look about him. He was slumped over, his head resting on the table, one arm curled around a bottle. His hair fanned out around his head and onto the table. He was wearing a filthy pair of orange Converse sneakers and a matching filthy scarf. I leaned against the booth and looked at him. Of all my Resistance contacts, Leo was my least favorite. He was brainwashed by his own I.Q., which he said was well above average. Supposedly his habits had gotten him kicked out of an Ivy League school, but I don't know if any of that was true. I do know that he thought he was smarter than everyone else. He even thought he was smarter than the drugs he took, like they wouldn't have an effect on him if he understood what they were doing to his body. Whatever. I couldn't stand him.

I craned my neck to get a look at the label on the bottle. Vodka. Good. No drugs. It was nice to see that he'd stayed off the hard stuff for my sake. I reached over, grabbed his shoulder and shook him. His head popped off the table.

"Can I help you?" His voice was clear, indignant and sober. Leo was the kind of punk who could pull it together in an instant. He couldn't hold it together long, but man, could he pull it together.

"Hi Leo." I slid into the booth.

"Madam you have me at a disadvantage. You are —?"

I crossed my arms. He was always fucking with me. We went

through this every damn time we met in person. I knew I should give in, just say the passphrase immediately, but I just couldn't let Leo have his way. I took out my phone and checked the time. "You know who I am."

Leo blinked. There was a crease across one of his cheeks, where he'd been resting his face on his arms. "I'm sure we've never met."

I leaned across the table. The bottle of vodka was more than half empty, but if I hadn't been able to smell him sweating out the alcohol, I would have sworn that he'd been holding onto that bottle for a friend.

"Leo, it is almost four in the morning. I twisted my ankle coming over here. I'm not in the fucking mood."

Leo's eyes narrowed. "Madam, you are disturbing my rest. Will I have to call the bouncer?"

I sighed and looked back down at my phone. It buzzed. Leo's number. I looked up at him and then back down at the phone. I brought up the message:

BAD SECRET AGENT. YOU LET ME GET BOTH HANDS UNDER THE TABLE.

This was followed by a winky emoticon.

My thumbs flew over the phone:

STOP BEING AN ASSHOLE. Smiley face.

There was a buzzing noise under his side of the table.

"I just texted you," I said. "There's your proof that you know me."

"It could be anyone," he said, looking down at his phone and looking back up at me, eyebrows raised. "I do have friends, and they have my phone number."

His fingers beat a tattoo on the touchscreen.

"Do they text you at 4 a.m.?"

"Why wouldn't they?"

My phone buzzed.

I looked down. JUST SAY IT. This was followed by an emoticon with one of those sideways Ps, Internet code for a tongue sticking out.

I looked up at him with narrowed eyes and sent the message I had already prepared: No.

When he looked up from his phone, I was making my own smiley face.

"Bouncer!" Leo's yell was so loud that the negotiating john and hooker jumped to their feet. "Bouncer! This woman is harassing me!"

The bouncer shambled over to us and looked down. "What? Her? She came in to see you. I thought you said you were waiting for someone."

I was texting furiously: WHAT. THE. FUCK. ARE. YOU. DOING.

Leo stood and glared at the bouncer. "Yes, her. I paid good money to take a nap in this booth and not to have women come in at almost four in the morning and disturb me."

"That don't make sense." The big man sighed. "You said you were waiting for someone. Here's someone." He pointed at me.

My phone buzzed.

SAY IT. Smiley face.

NO. Frowny face.

Leo looked at me. "She's not the someone I was waiting for. Just another hooker trying to make a buck off a guy. Get that gutter rat out of here."

"Oh, that's just ridiculous!" I shoved the table forward a few inches, so that it banged Leo in the legs. "Look at me!" I was wearing jeans and my long, black parka, one of those things that looks like the lovechild of a sleeping bag and a winter coat. "Do I look like a hooker to you?"

My phone buzzed again. I looked down.

WELL? ARE YOU GOING TO SAY IT?

I gave my head a slight shake.

"Come on. The pink hair, the tattoos. You look more like a prostitute than she does," Leo continued aloud. He pointed at the woman a few booths over. She glared at us. She looked old enough to be somebody's grandmother, but at least she had the decency to paint herself up like a whore.

"Whatever." The bouncer sighed and grabbed me by the elbow. "Come on, sister. Let's go."

He hauled me to my feet. I winced. "Wait a minute. What are you doing?"

He dragged me, hopping behind him, toward the door. The old barman watched with interest. Leo waved from his booth.

My phone buzzed. I looked down at it, while fighting to keep my ankle from hitting things.

HA HA.

I gritted my teeth and texted back, with one hand. Thank god for autocorrect or else it would have been gibberish: FINE. WILL SAY IT.

Leo came stumbling up to us just as the bouncer was about to toss me out. "Wait, wait." He waved his hands. "I think I *do* know her."

The bouncer let out a sigh and released my coat. I dropped six inches to the floor. My ankle took my weight. Lights began exploding in my head again. I stumbled against Leo.

"Say it," he hissed into my hair. The stink of his breath closed the back of my throat.

I pulled away. "This is stupid."

"Say it." Leo glanced at the bouncer, who was retreating to the bar.

I drew a breath in through my nose. We weren't supposed to say it unless we needed to say it. We were definitely not supposed to make a scene about saying it.

I dropped my head so that my face was practically in the collar of my parka. "The dove is fat, content and peaceful."

Leo was leering down at me, eyes wild with triumph. "I didn't hear you. A little bit louder, now."

I straightened my parka. "*No.* This is not a Chubby Checker song."

"Isley Brothers." Leo never threw away an opportunity to be a know-it-all. "'Shout' is an Isley Brothers song. Say it again."

I looked around. Everyone else had turned their attention back to whatever they had been doing. Except for the ancient barman, who was watching us idly. I turned my head in the other direction. "The dove is fat, content, and peaceful," I said.

"Beware the hawk." Leo said it too loudly, with relish, a little boy reciting a line from a spy movie. Then he spun on his heel and headed back to his booth.

"So," he said, when we'd resettled ourselves in his booth, "what took you so long?"

"I got the call late. They said that it might not even be here yet." I propped my ankle up on the seat opposite me.

"Well, they were right, as always. It is not here yet." He took a drink from the bottle. "You mentioned discomfort in your ankle. May I take a look at it? For your sake?"

Among other things, Leo claimed to have attended medical school.

I pulled my foot away from him. "When is it due to get here, and what do we do with it?"

"My masters have not seen fit to bestow that information on their humble servant," Leo said, beginning to slip into a strange highbrow Harvard-ish accent that I liked to think of as his Infuriating Voice. Tonight it was accompanied by Leo's Infuriating Face, which was an expression you might see if you caught an ivy-league professor in a whorehouse claiming to do research. The combination of face and voice were normally enough to make me violent. I was too tired to care.

"In that case, Leo, I would like to crash someplace until the package comes. I've been up all night."

"You can stay with me," he said.

"Oh, you have a place now, huh?" I spun my phone on the table in front of me. The motion made bubbles appear in different colors on the touchscreen. It was a useless app, but I liked it.

"I share it with some other renaissance men, such as myself," said Leo.

I guessed this meant that Leo was living in a crack house. I sighed. "I want the safehouse keys."

Leo rose up indignantly on his elbows, tried to look sober enough to be offended, failed and then tried again, with slightly more success.

"My dear, you do me a great injustice," said Leo. "My friends and I are gentlemen and gracious hosts."

"Leo," I smacked my palm on the table. "I'm too tired for this shit."

"Fine, my love, you can stay in the safehouse." He flipped me a key. "The address is on the label, in case you don't remember. I'll call you when I need you. Now, if you'll excuse me, I'm going to indulge in some Roman pleasures."

I left before I could find out whether he was talking about orgies, vomitoriums, or feeding Christians to lions.

People think working for the Resistance is glamorous, but let me tell you, it's not. I've been working for them for five years, and I still don't even know what the Resistance is. I know it's classified as a terrorist group or whatever, but it's not like I even do anything interesting for them. I'm a courier. Once a month, I take the bus or the train up to Boston and pick something up or drop it off. Sometimes I get to make a drop in D.C. or Philly. One time they sent me to Newark, and I seriously hope they never do that again. But the rest of the time? I'm an artist. I do installations in the city. I get a lot of tattoos. I go to a lot of bars. And — my roommates totally hate me for this — I don't have to have a job. The Resistance pays me. I get a check every month, and it's pretty decent cash. It kinda has to be, because I'm not allowed to have another job. The Resistance likes to have access to me at all times.

There are other perks. Like the iPhone. Every year I've been in the Resistance, I get a brand new cell phone in the mail. The first few years they were just regular phones, but after that, brand new iPhones. And the best part is that they're a little different than everybody else's iPhones. You can't get my iPhone in stores. It came pre-hacked, so you can run all kinds of apps on them. And here's the weird thing: You can't turn them off.

And you can't just leave that shit on a park bench or let the battery run down. I lost my phone once. I don't know where the hell I lost it; it just slipped out of my hoodie. It was duct taped to the outside of my bedroom window the next morning. The alarm kept going off. I know. Fuckin' creepy. I get the feeling that if I ever lost it again, I'd wake up with it duct taped to my face.

I couldn't get a cab. Cabs don't seem to run in Chinatown at 4 a.m. In the end, I had to gimp the half mile to Dorchester. On a nice day, it seemed like a short walk, but in December in the middle of the night, it seemed like forever. I managed to hit on a way of walking that didn't hurt so bad — I just sort of put the weight on my heel more than my toes — but it took forever, and I was tired and the streets were dark as hell.

It was a couple weeks before Christmas, but people had unplugged their strings of lights. In New York, the lights are on all day and all night and into the spring. Nobody turns anything off in New York. But in Boston? Please. Everything gets turned off at night. The subway — sorry, the T — the bars, even the Christmas lights. I wanted to get home to New York, where people were still moving around, and the streets weren't so lonely. I clutched my parka around me and flipped the hood up to hide my pink hair. Boston always made me feel less safe.

I don't like Boston much. Maybe it's because my younger sister lives here. She's got some PR job and a boyfriend or something and lives off the Green Line, don't ask me where. I picture her living in some yuppie brownstone, but it's probably just a regular apartment building. She has a cat, because that's what 22-year-olds who work in PR and live with their boyfriends do. They get "rescue cats." "Rescue cat," what a self-aggrandizing term. Like the cat was tied to the tracks of the Green Line and my sister came swooping down on it to save its life. I wonder how the cat feels about it. I wonder if it feels like it's been rescued. Maybe it would rather hang out in a dumpster in the alley and fuck other cats all day, rather than sitting in the window, neutered, eating all the Iams it can get. My sister would say that the cat is safe in the apartment. She's always thought very highly of safety. When we were little kids, she got nervous when I climbed too high in trees, or when I pushed her too hard on the swing. She never realized that living safely isn't really living.

The safehouse loomed in front of me. It was this dilapidated townhouse-looking thing. Tonight, it seemed completely made of stairs: steps from the sidewalk to the front door, and then three flights of stairs up to the apartment. I sighed and began to climb, slowly, using the railing to drag myself up, until I was standing in front of the apartment door.

The safehouse is neither safe nor a house. It's a one-bedroom apartment in Dorchester. I'd stayed there before and found it in varying states of disrepair each time, so I didn't know what to expect when I pushed the door open. It swung inward. I took a deep breath. It didn't stink. That was good. It didn't sound like anybody else was in there. That was *very* good.

I took a step forward into the room. The floor squeaked. Then something brushed my face. I squawked, and for a couple of seconds, I flapped my hands around in front of me until my fingers closed on a chain. Oh right. I remembered and pulled down on the chain. A bare bulb clicked on above me. The room in which I was standing had as its main furnishings an old couch, an armchair, a TV table and an old television. A kitchenette stood in the corner.

I poked my head around a corner and pulled a few more chains. The bedroom was empty except for a small cot. The bathroom was empty except for a space heater. I was alone. I sighed, shut the open door to the hallway, tossed my backpack onto the couch, and sat down. I pulled off my boots, carefully. My ankle was swollen to twice its regular size. I needed some ice but there was nothing in the freezer.

In every city I'd ever traveled to, there were apartments like these — small, furnished, sometimes nicely, sometimes horrible, rat-infested holes — but in every city there were safehouses. Yet in every city, no operative knew anyone but the person he or she had been put in touch with. I gimped into the bedroom. I didn't even bother to take my clothing off or shut off the light.

Ringtone. Ugh. I reached for the phone, which was on top of my blankets, somewhere. Light was blazing through the window. I peered at the damn thing. Leo was calling me and it was 8:30 in the morning.

Four hours of sleep. Christ. I moved a little. My ankle ached.

"What?" I held the phone to my ear.

"I got a call." Leo didn't sound so hot either. "The guy will be making the drop in an hour at the fountain on the Commons. Be there."

It was bright but cold. It hadn't snowed yet in Boston, which was a shame, because a little snow goes a long way toward making a city look prettier. Especially around Christmas time. Right now, despite the fact that there were garlands and lights all over the damn place, it didn't feel like the Christmas season at all. It just felt like an extension of November.

Leo and I sat on a bench near the fountain at the Boston Commons. The fountain is one of the most prominent landmarks in Boston's best-known park. It's right next to the city's most touristy subway station. Normally we meet *in* subway stations, not near them. People were hurrying in and out, headed to work or to school or to the Freedom Trail or wherever normal people go at 9:30 a.m. on a weekday morning in Boston. I couldn't imagine why the Resistance contact asked us to meet here. We were seated with a collection of vagrants on the benches around the fountain, which was dry for the winter. More than I can say for Leo. He was nursing his hangover with a flask. Business types on phones, bundled-up tourists, and one very determined t-shirt salesman milled around our bench. I turned my glare on Leo. He was pale; the vodka didn't seem to have agreed with him, so at least he was quiet. He just sat there, eyeing the group around the fountain for his contact. Every couple of seconds he would start up off the bench as if he'd spotted him and then sink back down, disappointed. He fidgeted a lot. Then he began jogging his knee and shaking the bench. The movement was hurting my ankle. I shot him a look, which he didn't catch. Hanging out with Leo was a lot like being told that you had to mind a kindergarten class for an hour.

I checked my phone: 9:50. The Resistance had never kept me waiting before, and I sure as hell never kept the Resistance waiting. Pick-ups were private, prompt, and easy. You know, you get a text to meet a guy in a blue hat in the third car of the MetroNorth Train to New Haven when it passes through Harrison, New York. Then he gets off in one stop, you get off in two, go to the other side of the station, and take the train back to Grand Central. Easy peasy. No problemo. But this was weird.

I shifted my bad ankle. *Okay*, I thought, *I don't like Leo. But this is his territory, and it's his contact. He should know whether this is normal or not. I need to trust him.*

Leo started up out of his seat again as a man walked by, then sighed and plopped back down. The bench started vibrating again.

A few minutes later, an old man, dressed in rags and smelling ripe, hobbled over to us and gestured to the pigeons. "The birds are pretty," he mumbled. "Feed the birds, the birds are pretty."

Everyone stared idly at him as he shambled around and around the fountain, birds scattering in front of him, muttering "fat bird, pretty bird." I was rooting in my pockets for change to give him, when, to my left, I heard a loud "Beware the hawk!"

I stared at Leo, who had leapt to his feet. Everyone was staring at us. Leo rushed toward the alarmed-looking old man, and hustled him out of sight, behind one of the subway terminals, leaving me sitting alone while all the other vagrants leered at me.

"Hey pink," said one guy, who was clutching a greasy paper bag. He grinned at me. I counted three visible teeth. "That your boyfriend?"

"Yeah, sure, he's the love of my life. Fuck off," I said.

A couple of the guys hooted. I stared off after Leo. I couldn't believe it. I mean, fine, the old man might be a master of disguise, but he didn't even have the correct password. I looked around, but Leo and the bum were nowhere to be seen, and now people were looking at me, and that's a big no-no. Not as big a no-no as getting the wrong guy though. That shit gets you disappeared. At least, that's what I've heard.

I checked my phone. If he wasn't back in five minutes, I would text him. I winced. That's like the least bad-ass spy-type thing I could do, ever. I tried to picture James Bond turning to his Bond Girl of the moment and saying, "If I'm not back in 15 minutes, text."

Whatever. I had to admit to myself that no one sitting by the fountain would have made a better contact than the old man. All of them were just as wasted-away, grimy, and wore approximately the same vacant expressions. I sat back. Leo must have the right one. I sat there, trying to empty my mind like they teach you to do in yoga class, until he came back, alone.

"Well?" I looked pointedly at his hands. They were empty.

"He's a tough nut to crack," he mused, sitting back down on the bench. "I tried everything to convince him that I am trustworthy."

My blood felt like it was starting to boil. "Leo, I thought this man was your contact. You don't know what he looks like?"

Leo's Infuriating Face made an appearance. "Why, *of course* I don't what he looks like," he chuckled, patting me on the arm. "I don't know what kind of shoddy operation you run in Brooklyn, but here, we hardly *ever* meet our contacts in the open. He and I have spoken on the phone, through a distorter."

I felt my chest get tight.

"Leo," I was trying to whisper, but it came out as a croak, "you stupid *fuck*. You got the wrong guy."

Leo favored me with a superior smile. "Look," he said, using his Infuriating Voice, "there's no need to get childish with me because I criticized your operation in Brooklyn."

"I'm not being childish — you fucked it up. Do you know what happens when we fuck something up?" I felt like I was on the brink of hyperventilation.

"No," said Leo, grabbing me by the shoulders and looking straight into my eyes. "Because I've never fucked anything up. Now listen to me. You are overreacting. Yes, this meeting was unorthodox. Yes, things are a bit uncertain here, and no, we don't have the package, but my dear, you have to trust me. This is my territory. I know how the system works here. We just need to give this guy some more time. He'll open up eventually; I know he will. We'll come back tomorrow at the same time, and he'll make the drop."

"And if he's not the right guy?" I was nearly in tears. "Leo, is it possible that you've made a mistake?" As soon as it left my lips, I knew it was the wrong thing to say.

Leo chuckled patronizingly.

"Love, I never make mistakes."

I turned and headed off into the crowd on the street. If he wanted me, he could text me.

I limped though the crowded streets at Downtown Crossing, clutching a latte. My ankle was killing me. I needed to find a drug store, get some aspirin or something. Maybe even a bandage or an ice pack, but all I could find in this section of town were department stores and Starbucks.

The pain and the panic were making me nauseous. Somewhere, down in the twisted depths of his ego, even Leo had to know that something was wrong. Well, I thought, if something was indeed wrong, it was Leo's fault. Therefore, Leo would have to pay for it. I knew better than that, though. It was my mission, and I would pay as well. Shit.

What remained of my bus ticket from New York was still in my pocket. I fingered it for a second. A fetid mirage of the return trip rose before me: sticky Fung-Wah floors, livestock on the bus, loud arguments in Chinese, the Mass Pike rushing away beneath me, an orange train surfacing briefly beside the Pike, like a big metal worm, bound for Jamaica Plains. Chickens and passengers screaming as the bus's air conditioner caught on fire and smashed into an oil tanker. The vision dissolved quickly, and I pushed the desire to disobey orders to the back of my mind.

Shit. *Shit.* That was it. I was going back to bed. I wasn't going to get up, either. Not until Leo called me with the correct information or somebody showed up to shoot me. That was all I could do.

I hobbled into the Downtown Crossing train station and inhaled the communal halitosis of the subway. I loved the idea of subways; they were secretive and dark; there were roped off subterranean passages and abandoned tracks and stations neglected by generations of city governments. Somehow though, the reality of the subways always disgusted me; layers of spit on the ground and the general reek of humanity, packed in boxes and belched out onto slimy platforms to breathe in each other's gases.

The air on the platform was humid. I was trying to find a place to ditch my latte when I heard the sound of air being pushed through the tunnel at the end of the platform. The red line train streaked by me, and I caught blurry glimpses of the people in the cars as the train rolled in and slowed down. A pair of doors shuddered to a halt right in front of me. I squared myself before them, waiting to fight the rush of people that would push out of the car. The doors whooshed open. I stuck out my elbows, gritted my teeth, and found myself looking directly into the big, brown eyes of Danny Nulty.

I blinked.

He blinked back, above the heads of all the other passengers. I never expected to see Danny again. In fact, I was startled that I remembered him.

We'd met a year before at the counter of a Starbucks near Quincy Market. I dropped my stirrer; he smiled. He took me out for a beer the same night, but that was it. He never called, and I was not really surprised. Danny was too decent. He loved dogs, kids, America, and the Red Sox. During our one date, he stopped twice to give money to homeless people on the street. He told me he wanted to be a cop, but couldn't make the Academy, and settled for a job at his uncle's auto body shop instead.

Right now, his huge, handsome face was grinning crookedly at me. Even though I was still freaking out over the Leo thing, it was hard not to grin back. If I weren't the kind of girl who carried other people's pipe bombs in her purse, maybe I would have made more of an effort at dating Danny.

He pushed through the people in the subway car to give me an awkward half-hug. "Sweetheart!" He pronounced it *sweet-haht*, "How you doin'?"

"I'm all right." I fidgeted with the coffee cup I'd never managed to get rid of. "What are you up to?"

"Nothing much — getting ready for spring training." He smiled in that maybe-the-Sox-have-a-chance-this-year kind of way. "What are you doing in Beantown, sweetheart? Here on business?"

Danny didn't know what my business was, but he did know that it was the reason I came to Boston.

I nodded. The subway jolted, and I was knocked off balance, so that my weight fell onto my ankle. I gasped and pitched sideways.

Danny reached out and steadied me. "Woah, sweetheart. What's going on with your foot?"

"It's nothing. I just sprained it a little yesterday. That's all." His hand was on my waist. I could feel it through the parka.

"Wearing those high-heeled shoes, huh?" Danny chuckled. "I'll never understand women."

I smiled. If I looked like the kind of girl who marched around in pumps, I had failed to make my desired fashion statement.

"Where are you off to?" The subway rocked. I steadied myself against him.

"Oh," Danny grinned and shook his head. "I'm just doing an errand for the old man. But later I'm going to meet some friends near Quincy Market for a beer." His eyes lit up a little, and he leaned down to look at me. "Wanna come, angel?"

I began to mumble something about having plans, but partway through my excuse, I looked up and saw those warm, brown eyes, and I realized that his hand was still at the small of my back. I smiled. "Where?"

"The Purple Shamrock, six thirty."

The train was slowing down. This was going to be my stop.

"See you, sweetheart," he called as I fought my way out of the train.

He *did* say that he would be at the bar at six thirty. I glared at my iPhone. It was seven.

I shifted on my barstool and kept my eyes fixed on the door. My foot was propped on a chair, but I had a lot of reasons to be uncomfortable. There are places in Boston where pink hair is common, but I wasn't sitting in one of them. I was getting lots of interesting looks from the Purple Shamrock's khaki-clad clientele.

I love my hair. It's a bob, with bangs, and it's a really, *really* bright pink. I actually had it dyed to match my iPhone case, and I've got a coordinated pink and black tattoo on my back. It's all pink and black flowers. It started as a tramp stamp but kind of took over. One of my roommates calls it a tramp stampede. I wanted to get one of those microdermal transplants on my face, to match, just a little pink jewel where a beauty spot would be, but the last thing I need is trouble when I go through metal detectors.

I sat in a shadowy corner, keeping an eye on the door and jumping every time I saw a guy who looked like Danny. I jumped a lot. If we were friends on Facebook, or if I even had his number, I could have texted him, but no dice. By the time the fifteenth curly-headed, Irish guy in a cable-knit sweater passed me, I was getting ready to get ready to give Danny ten more minutes before I left the bar.

He saved me the trouble by careening through the Purple Shamrock doors, looking as if he he'd just gotten out of the shower. His hair was damp, he was recently shaven and he had done a rather hasty job of tucking his blue button-down into his khakis. He came right over to me.

"Hey, sweetheart, been here long?" he said breathlessly and bent down to kiss my cheek. He smelled like soap and Old Spice.

"Not that long," I lied. "Wow. You're good — you spotted me over here in the shadows."

Danny grinned and pointed at my head. "You're kinda hard to miss, angel. You look like that chick from *The Fifth Element*."

I shook my head and laughed. "She had orange hair."

Danny smiled. "Yeah." He leaned down and looked in my eyes. "But you're both hot."

The closer he got, the more my body responded. I blushed.

Danny straightened up. "Tell you what. You keep off that foot. Let me go get you a drink." He gestured toward the bar. "I'm really sorry I'm late. It was a busy day in work today."

"A lot of work at the garage?"

Danny smiled and rubbed my back. "Sweetheart," he said. "We have *got* to catch up."

And then we were descended upon. "Danny! Oh my *god*! I haven't seen you in, like, for*ever*!"

He didn't mention that his friends were female.

I turned my head to see three skinny girls wearing black tank tops and khakis. Danny picked all of them up in one gigantic hug and then dropped them. They fell on their feet, three Siamese cats, styled by Abercrombie & Fitch.

"Sweetheart," he said, "This is Corinne, Marisa and Marcy. College friends. We went to Northeastern together."

Of course they did.

The girls were hard to shake and very talkative. As I couldn't help but find out, they all lived comparatively normal lives. I zoned in and out of their little worries, alternately listening and looking at the door. Some date. I kept my hand in my pocket. My phone was on vibrate. If it rang, I was outta here.

"Sweetheart, you've got to hear this." Danny snapped me out of my reverie to listen to an "epic" story about Marisa nearly getting caught with a joint in college.

"I threw it out the window right before the RA came in," she said. "God knows what would have happened if they caught me."

I smiled. I know what would have happened if they caught her. The RA might have written her up. Maybe if her parents were hard-asses, they would take her car away over Thanksgiving break. Ooh. Scary.

I had that life too, once. It sucked. There was a time when the only authorities I really worried about were students a few years ahead of me, or my family. I felt a familiar knot in my stomach. I really had been afraid of my family, although God knows, Mom and Dad were never much in the disciplinary department. They didn't seem to give a crap when I dropped out of the college they were spending so much money on and moved away, cutting off contact with no explanation. They never tried to find out what was going on.

I remembered the day, five years ago, that I packed up my dorm room, pulled out of school and joined the Resistance. I'd found them on Craigslist. No joke. The ad was pretty impressive. Power to the people and all that, invoking the Weathermen and the Black Panthers, and revolutionaries like Fidel Castro and Che Guevara. Young rebels, leaving their lives of privilege to serve the people, or whatever. I was sacrificing my own education to serve the masses. I didn't know what I was joining, exactly, but it seemed like a better idea than liberal arts. And the ad promised $50k per year as a starting wage. I signed up without knowing anything.

I know how dumb all of this sounds. But for me, it was heaven. All of a sudden I'm making $50,000 a year and I don't have to do anything for it? Screw college. Screw my parents. Because if I'm making $50k for nothing that means I never have to ask my family for anything, and if I never have to ask my family for anything, that means I don't have to speak to them ever again.

"Angel?" Danny shouted in my ear. "Are you all right?"

I nodded. The girls were gone, gyrating on the makeshift dance floor. The music was deafening. I fingered my phone in my pocket. I probably should leave.

"Sweetheart," he yelled. "How long are you here for this time? You don't really come to Boston that often, do you?"

"I don't know," I screamed. "Whenever they send me back, I guess I'm leaving."

"Who are 'they'?" He shouted this into my face, but in a nice way. "You never even told me what you do."

I guessed this was going to be coming. "What? Sorry, can't hear you," I yelled.

Danny shook his big head and pushed back from the table. "I'll get us another round," he screamed and ambled off toward the bar

I looked down at my phone. The pumping bass made it difficult to tell if it had been vibrating. I had a missed call. The number was blocked. I needed to get out of this bar. I looked up for Danny and couldn't find him in the crush at the bar. I hated to ditch him, but I needed to get outside.

The phone buzzed in my hand. I looked down. There was a text from a blocked number: I SEE YOU.

The next couple of minutes were a blur of motion. I was out of that bar like a shot, tripping over clubbers, my ankle throbbing.

I galloped across the street to the City Hall Plaza, cursing in the cold. It occurred to me that I could be overreacting. Maybe the texter was Leo. Maybe he was fucking with me again. Maybe he somehow found out I had a date and came here to ruin my night. Leo did stuff like that. Or maybe it was the contact we'd missed this morning, come to give me the item so I could get the fuck out of Beantown and go the hell home. I made for the dark side of City Hall. If it was a new contact from the Resistance, that would be a good place to talk — the drunken masses used the plaza on the other side of City Hall to get to the subway.

I hobbled up the steps and ducked into the shadowy, post-modern recesses of City Hall's facade. It was a modern building, designed in the style of *Star Trek: Next Generation* set pieces. Obviously, its architect had giddy hopes of bringing Boston from Bunker Hill to the Final Frontier with his bold design, but really, the building was just ugly.

The sound of footsteps echoed off the building. Maybe whoever it was would just run on by. Except that he didn't. The footsteps stopped right in front of my enclave.

I stuck my face out from the shadows. There was a man there, a slight guy I'd never met, wearing khakis and a fleece. He had a goatee.

"Are you here to talk?" I asked, limping out into the light. "Maybe to discuss fat, peaceful doves?"

He looked down at my ankle. "You're hurt."

"Yeah? So?" I started to edge away from the wall.

I at least made it into the open air of the frozen plaza before his fist grazed my head.

Now, this might sound stupid, but I don't fight. I'm a courier for Christ's sake. I carry shit around for people. I mean, the last fight I got in was with my sister when I was 16 and she was 13. I won that fight, by the way. I just didn't think that I'd be able to win this particular one. He knew I wasn't even going to be able to run.

So what's a slightly-tipsy, injured spy girl to do? Well, hell, they do it in the movies. I went for his neck.

Epic fail. He was too fast for me. His arm whizzed past me again, and I spun to the side. The world spun with me. I stopped in time to see that a leg was in my way. I tripped-hopped over it, and my ankle burned with pain.

Fucked, I thought as his arm came flying past again, *I'm fucked.*

Something in his glove was glinting. A knife. This guy was definitely here on business. I saw something else glitter. His teeth. He was smiling. He lunged again. I threw my hand out in front of me to protect my face, like I used to do when I was playing sports in gym class and the ball was coming right at me. Good way to lose a finger, right? But I got lucky. His neck connected with my fist.

He reeled backwards, clutching at his windpipe. I stood there, shocked at my own accidental bad-assery, listening to him gasp. The knife clattered to the ground. I remembered all the action movies I'd ever seen and kicked it as far from him as I could, which wasn't far.

He was gurgling and coughing, and something heavier fell to the pavement from his fleece. A gun. Who keeps that in his pocket? I realized I was shaking. Fuck my ankle; I should run. *I really should do that*, I thought.

"What the hell is going on here?" a male voice echoed off City Hall.

We both froze, and then the man who was not Leo took off, running back down the stairs toward the crowds of Fanueil Hall, leaving his gun and knife on the ground. He leapt down the stairs and disappeared from view.

"Hey, where the fuck do you think you're going?" the other voice shouted, and I heard two sets of footsteps scuffling on the landing below. I didn't want to look. I didn't want to face whoever else might be headed up to my frozen, little plateau. I just wanted to get the hell out of there. I made a move to leave and my foot knocked against something. I jumped and looked down.

The gun was near my feet. I bent down and picked it up. It was lighter than I thought it would be. I'd never held one. I lifted it up so I could see it. It was plastic; it was almost a shock when I realized it was real. It looked like a really good child's toy, from back when I was a kid, before toy guns had those silly plastic tips. There was something written on it. It looked like "lock." I looked more carefully. Glock.

I heard more yelling and scuffling. I needed to go. I dropped the gun into my messenger bag and began limping as fast as I could toward the subway station. My knees felt like they might give out. I didn't want to go back to the safehouse, but couldn't think where else I should go.

"Wait right there." It was the second voice. I froze. Here we go. I breathed as deeply as I could in the cold air, trying to figure out whether it would be better to run or to stay where I was and get caught by…what? A Resistance killer? A cop? A mugger?

"Sweetheart? Is that you?" I turned to see Danny, puffing up the flight of concrete stairs behind me. He wasn't wearing a coat, but he was sweating profusely. "You okay? What the hell is going on? You run off, then there's that asshole down there. "You all right? What did he do? Mug you?"

"I'm fine," I said in a voice that didn't sound like anything I could recognize. "I just need to go home."

Danny approached me and took me by the shoulders. He gave me a long, hard look. "Home? You okay? You look pale as hell. Did he hurt you?"

"Did you catch him?" I couldn't believe I was asking this. I was the spy with the Glock in my bag. He was a mechanic.

Danny sighed and pulled me into a hug. His button down was damp against my cheek. "No," he said. "He got away from me, angel. I'm sorry."

I closed my eyes and inhaled his scent. Just being close to Danny calmed me down. I was reminded less of previous boyfriends, and more of my dad, picking me up when I was little, telling me it was going to be okay, and me believing him, even though it never was.

"Jesus." Danny pushed me away from him suddenly. "Is that a knife?" He stalked over to the knife and knelt over it. He looked on the verge of picking it up with a handkerchief, TV cop style.

"Well, yeah." I shoved my hands into my parka. Without Danny to hold onto, I was suddenly cold.

Danny looked up at me. "Looks like he didn't get your bag."

This was getting to be ridiculous. I shrugged. "What, so I'm supposed to let some whacko rob me? I'm a big girl; I punched him in the throat. He dropped the knife." Man, I sounded tough. "And," I added, impressed by myself, "I think the guy had a gun."

"You punched a guy in the throat?" Danny smiled and shook his head. "Right. Sweetheart, if he had a gun, why did he hold you up with a knife?"

I stood there like I'd been slapped. I hadn't thought of that.

"Come on, big girl," he said, laughing and putting his arm around me. "I'm taking you home."

"Home? What? Back to New York?" I pulled away from him, trying to joke my way out of this.

"Wherever you're staying." He took a step closer. "Where do you stay when you're in town, anyways? You got a hotel? I can take you there."

"Danny, no. I can make it back by myself." I stepped back. "You don't have to escort me."

"Yes I do. Christ," he said. "You can barely walk. Come here." He reached down and before I could stop him, lifted me off the ground.

"Very funny," I said. "Let me down."

"It's okay. You don't weigh anything," he said, even though I said nothing about my weight. "It's a good thing you forgot to give me your phone number."

"Hmm?" I was looking over his shoulder, trying to see if the guy in the fleece was still lurking in the shadows.

"You ran out of the bar on me without giving me your number," he said, and carried me over the turnstile and into the T station.

"It's okay," he said to the attendant who hurried out. "She hurt her foot." Then he carefully carried me through the crowd and placed me on a train.

I knew better than this. The rules about this sort of thing were clear. You don't let civilians into the safehouse. You don't let them escort you "home." You don't tell them which subway lines to take or point out the streets that need to be walked down in order to get there. I knew all that. But I was shaken up. I was tired. I was terrified. My ankle throbbed. Just then, all I wanted was for someone to sweep in and take care of me. I was weak. I'm not proud of it.

"We're going to Dorchester," I told him.

We were quiet for the whole ride, wedged next to one another in those tiny plastic seats. I kept my bag on my lap and my eye on the reflections in the subway windows. At every stop, I searched the heads in the crowd for anyone who looked like my attacker, but my attention kept taking a detour, either to the shape of the gun in my bag or to the heat of Danny's thigh against my own. The subway was crowded, and we were jammed next to one another, connected along the sides of our body, from the knees to the hips. I tried to focus on a plan. I'd need to have a place to go after he dropped me off at the safehouse. I sure as hell wouldn't be able to stay there tonight, or if I did, I would need to shoot that attacker when he came through the door. Shooting the attacker seemed like the best idea, actually. If I barricaded myself in, if no one was already there, waiting for me...

Danny shifted his thigh, and the plan fell apart in my head.

"Our stop, angel," he murmured.

I was glad to see the safehouse. I'd insisted on walking from the subway station and my ankle throbbed.

"Okay, well, you got me here," I said, making a big show about taking out my key. "Thanks for the escort home."

Danny didn't move.

"Okay," I turned, my hand on the doorknob and gave him a big smile, "good night."

"I'm coming in," he said. I turned. He climbed the steps from the sidewalk and stood close to me. I had all kinds of reasons I didn't want him in the safehouse, but on the other hand, it seemed like a good idea to get him to come in. He'd tangled with the guy in the fleece, which might be enough to get him noticed by the Resistance. And the neighborhood was kind of rough. I knew I wouldn't be able to live with myself if he was attacked on his way home. Yeah, he was a big guy, but he was also just a regular civilian. I felt like he'd be safer with me. Also, I can't lie; while he was standing there, so close I could feel his body heat, all I could think to say was "Okay."

He followed me, closely, into the building and up the stairs, and stood behind me as I fumbled with the apartment door.

"You have a tattoo on your neck," he said. His breath ruffled the hair at the base of my neck. My skin puckered. I never let guys get to me like this. Why it was happening right when both of us could get shot, I didn't know.

"Yeah." I jammed my key into the apartment door and moved away from him, into the darkness of the apartment, trying to put a little distance between us. I had to concentrate. There might be someone in here. I sniffed the darkness. It didn't smell different, but my nostrils were full of Danny's scent, ten times stronger than it had in City Hall Plaza. I reached for the chain to turn on the light and realized I'd overshot it by about a foot. Goddamn. My hands were shaking. I pictured an intruder watching our outlines in the door, leveling a gun at my head. Any minute now, bang, and we'd both be dead. I needed to be able to see. I backed up to turn on the lights and nearly screamed when I slammed into someone.

"How far down does it go?" Danny's hands slipped under my parka and onto my hips. I breathed in, jaggedly, reached up and turned on the light. The bulb snapped on. The apartment looked empty. I could see into the kitchenette and the living room and the bathroom, more or less. I couldn't see into the bedroom.

"Woah. What is this place?" Danny's voice was just at my ear. "Does one of your friends live here or something?"

"Yeah, something like that," I shifted my weight so that my bad ankle wasn't bearing so much of it. "How far down does what go?" I tried to take a step forward, but his hands had crept around my hips and were sliding down the tops of my thighs.

"The tattoo." Danny was murmuring into my neck now. My knees were weak. I stared off in the direction of the bedroom.

With an effort, I extricated myself. "Would you excuse me for a minute? I have to go drop this in the bedroom."

Danny shut the door behind him with one hand. "Let me come with you." His voice was warm and rough, he was untucking his shirt with the other hand. I tried, and failed, to keep my eyes above his belt. I closed my eyes and swallowed.

"Just have a seat," I pointed at the sofa, "and I'll be right out, okay?"

"Sure." Danny headed toward the couch, and I went into the bedroom, slowly, hand in my messenger bag, on the gun inside. I heard a loud curse in the living room. I had forgotten to warn him about the couch spring. I stepped just into the room, and flicked on the light. Nothing. I pulled the closet door open and looked behind it. I pulled off my parka, and sat down on the cot to unlace my boots. I rubbed my ankle. Sweat was running down my torso, and I knew it wasn't just because I'd been afraid of an intruder. Now I was reasonably sure we were alone in the apartment. All alone. It felt like there was a spring coiling tightly behind my belly button.

I'm not a prude or anything, I've fucked my fair share of guys. Resistance guys, regular guys, older guys, younger guys. I almost fucked Leo once when I was drunk. No big deal, right? But no guy had managed to get under my skin like this. Sweet fucking Jesus.

If this were a regular night, I thought, and I weren't terrified that some crazed Resistance operative was going to let himself in and start knifing us, I'd go out there right now and fuck Daniel's brains out.

"Sweetheart," he called from the living room, "you coming out or what?"

I took a deep breath. What a way to go.

I peeled off my t-shirt and bra, loosened my belt and opened the bedroom door. "You want to know how far down the tattoo goes?" I walked into the living room, stepping out of my jeans on the way. This time Danny sucked in his breath. It's an amazing tattoo. It starts at the nape of my neck and goes all the way down. Then it comes right back up the front.

I stopped in front of the couch and pulled off my panties.

"Holy shit." He stood up and reached out to trace the swirls around a nipple.

I pushed his hands aside, grabbed his shoulders, and pulled myself up onto him, wrapping one of my legs around one of his.

Danny put those big hands under my ass and lifted me up. I wrapped my legs around his waist. "Holy shit," he said again.

He was breathing heavily. I felt the material of his shirt moving against my breasts.

"Shut up," I said and forced my tongue into his mouth. He fell backward, dragging me down onto the couch. That stupid spring grazed my shin when we landed.

I'll be honest. The foreplay was way better than the actual sex. It always is, the first time. With Danny and me, there only was that first time.

"Never had a girl with racing stripes," he'd said, later, before drifting off to sleep on the cot.

"It's body art," I said, wriggling out from under one of his arms.

"Racing stripes." His laugh was sleepy. "Fast. Sexy. Vroom."

"Fine. Racing stripes." I picked up my shirt, coat and messenger bag. He was already snoring. There really wasn't enough room on the cot for both of us. I'd be sleeping on the couch, facing the door, with the Glock and my iPhone.

* * *

Danny was still asleep when I woke up the next morning. I could hear him snoring as I showered, got dressed and let myself out of the apartment. I tried to wake him, but he just snorted and rolled over when I shook him. He was too big to move, and there was no food, so I slipped out. I was only planning to leave him alone there for a few minutes. When the door shut behind me, it was 9 a.m.

The paranoia from the night before had lifted. I'd woken up like nothing was wrong, grinning like an idiot, like I hadn't been attacked the night before, and like there was no gun in my messenger bag. I had this insane desire to make him breakfast, eggs and bacon, you know, fuck food. But there was nothing in the kitchen, and so I decided to just go down to the corner grocery store instead for a cup of coffee and whatever they had there. Maybe they had ACE bandages, or ice packs. My ankle was still killing me.

It was a sunny, cold day. People were rushing around me on the sidewalks. Rushing to work, rushing to class. Let them rush. I didn't have to go to anywhere. Not until my phone rang. I walked into the little mom and pop grocery place down the street and poured myself a cup of coffee at the counter. The windows of the place were greasy, but that was fine; the crap on the window made the sunlight streaming through look gold, like in an art house movie or in those Instagram photos you can take with your phone. The floor was dirty, too, but I don't mind that kind of thing. I like these little places. They made me feel like people still have souls. There was a canary hanging behind the counter and a cat hanging out on top of a case of soda. The supermarkets where I'm from would not be cool with that. There would be lawsuits and complaints, visits from inspectors. That was what I really gave up when I joined the Resistance. I gave up the floors you could eat off of, the lawns that looked like golf courses, the houses that looked like palaces but were really just shitty houses on steroids. I gave up people who talk about how important it was to have self-esteem and then run out to bleach their hair, change their noses and get new boobs. I gave up their kids, who rebelled against their platinum blonde mothers by sitting around chain coffee stores in designer pre-ripped jeans, scribbling bad poetry in those hardbound, moleskin notebooks. I figured that people would be more real in the underground. That was a disappointment. Look at Leo. There are pretentions every-fucking-where.

My iPhone rang while I was pushing the lid onto my coffee cup. A male voice was shrilling before I'd finished raising the phone to my ear.

"— you need to meet me now," it was saying. It took me a few seconds to identify the voice as Leo. I looked outside, just to double check that the sun was indeed up. He should be sleeping.

"Get to the bar," he said. "You need to meet me. We need to talk."

"Leo," I said. "It's nine in the morning. I'm not going to a bar." I was circling around the store's one aisle. No bandages. No ice packs. No aspirin.

Leo wasn't listening to me. "I fucked it up; I fucked up the drop. I didn't get the right guy," he stammered. "I just got a call from the Resistance. They're angry. Shit, they're angry."

Great. He got an angry phone call. I'd gotten attacked. I pulled one of those prepackaged, sugary Danish things off a rack and put it next to the coffee on the counter.

"No one came to see you?" The young woman behind the counter rang up my order on an ancient register.

"No. My god. Do you think they would come after us?"

"Never mind," The girl pointed at my total, and I dug around in the pockets of my parka for change. "What did they tell you?"

Leo slipped into a sort of hysterical monologue. "They said that the guy was there when we went to go pick up the package, but that I walked off with someone else. They accused us of talking to the cops. My god. They think that bird guy is a cop."

I wrestled some change out of my pocket and handed it to the girl behind the counter. She counted it and shook her head. I dug my hand back into my pocket, pulled out a twenty and slapped it down and limped out of the store, fast.

"I'm at Snowflower," he groaned. "You've got to get over here. They think we're trying to sell them out or something. They're going to kill us if we don't get this right. They say they're going to get in touch with us later, but dammit, we need to get this thing straightened out or we're dead."

"Fine." I hung up. I wanted to call Danny, but remembered that I didn't have his number. I started to hobble back toward the safehouse but stopped half a block in when I realized that it would take me twice as long to get to Chinatown if I doubled back. Danny would have to let himself out. I really didn't like leaving him there — I felt like I had a responsibility to Danny — but the drop was more important, and if I didn't make it, I'd be putting Danny, myself and Leo in more danger. Danny would be okay, I told myself and hobbled toward Chinatown. He would amble right out of the safehouse and right out of my life, and he would be fine.

It was probably just as well. I didn't need complications. Long-distance dating, hell, dating in general, and being in the Resistance didn't really go together. I didn't know it then, but when I joined the Resistance, I gave that up, too.

It took me a while to get to the bar. At 10:30 a.m. Leo was once again face-down in his favorite booth. There were a few bottles near his head this time. He looked like he was trying to pass out.

"Leo, wake the fuck up," I said.

He whimpered.

"Beware the fucking hawk, it's me. Get up. We have a lot of talking to do."

I noticed that the old bartender was watching us again and limped over to him. "Hey asshat," I leaned over the bartop, "don't you have dishes to wash or something?"

The old man scuttled off into the back room.

I returned to Leo's booth and lowered myself gingerly. "I didn't get into this business to yell at old men." I ripped into the Danish.

Leo stared at me. "Why did you?"

"Huh?" My mouth was full of Danish.

"Get into the business?" He poured himself a shot of something and threw it back miserably.

"I thought I'd be doing something good," I said. "For society."

Leo looked at me like I had three heads. "Why would you think that?"

"I don't know. That's what the Craigslist ad said," I said and bit another hunk out of the Danish. It was so sugary that it burned the back of my mouth. "And the money was good."

"Ah. Yes." Leo nodded. "The money is good. That's why I joined. Needed the cash."

I'll bet he did.

I stared at my coffee. "When did they say they were going to get in touch with us again?"

"They didn't say." Leo's voice fell back into a self-pitying whine. "They only said that they would contact us with further information when they knew what had happened to the bird guy."

"They're looking for the bird guy." I looked up at the bar's one reinforced window. I didn't expect that. This wasn't good. It sounded like the Resistance might have lost track of whatever it was I was supposed to be getting. I didn't like the idea of a jittery Resistance.

"Yeah," said Leo. "Apparently he just wandered away from the drop site, never to be seen again."

"Christ, Leo, for all we know, they might think we ran off with him and the package," I said.

"What do you think I'm so worried about?" Leo's Infuriating Voice began to infiltrate his panic. He threw back another shot and looked speculatively toward the back room. I shook my head. If he went into that opium den, I'd never get him out. I wondered if I should tell him about my attacker last night, about the knife and the gun and the anonymous text messages. I decided against it. At best, he'd freak out. At worst, he'd use the information to somehow fuck everything up even more. He'd screwed things up enough. I could barely look at him. God. All I had done was come to town to collect.

We sat waiting in the bar for hours. Finally, at 1 p.m. Leo's iPhone rang.

He walked away from our table and picked it up slowly, listened for a second and placed it in his pocket gingerly, as if he were afraid that it would break. He nodded at me. There wasn't much information. Our contact had either been found or replaced. We were going back to the Boston Common. I didn't ask if they'd found the bird guy.

It was early afternoon. And it was cold. At the Common, Leo and I sat side-by-side near the dry fountain, watching people run to and from the subway, trying to get out of the bitter cold. At 2:30, he turned to me, holding out a pack of Camels.

"Smoke?"

"Sure." I took one without looking at him.

He lit them, and, for a while, we just sat there in silence, listening to the intimate sound of the cigarette paper burning.

"You know I'm an asthmatic?" asked Leo, taking a drag.

"Why the fuck would I even care whether you're asthmatic or not?" I didn't look at him. There was a pause.

"You hate me, don't you?" asked Leo.

I turned. I had never heard him sound so plaintive.

"No Leo," I said. "I don't hate you. But you do piss me off sometimes."

Leo digested my response for a minute, studying the smoke as it left his allegedly-asthmatic lungs. "Well," he said, taking another drag, "I suppose that shows that you do, in fact, have a small mind — but there is hope for you."

I gritted my teeth. Maybe I did hate him.

Just then, a ragged man shuffled by us and sat with his back to the tree we had been watching. He was taller than the other bums and more powerfully built. His skin was the color of really dark coffee. I looked him up and down and noticed the care with which someone had made him look ratty. The coat he was wearing was ripped up but clean, as were his jeans, his gloves, and his hat, which wasn't nearly greasy enough for him to have been a real bum. His boots were still intact. He had a long roll of paper and sat by the tree as if he were waiting.

Leo jumped to his feet. "The pigeons remind me of doves; fat, content, and peaceful," he said, gesturing at the birds that flocked to the Common.

"Beware the hawk," the raggedy man intoned.

I hauled myself up and limped over.

"You're hurt," said the newcomer.

I nodded. I wished people would stop saying it like that, like I was the lame antelope in a Discovery Channel special about the hunting habits of lions.

Leo stared expectantly at the roll of paper. "Do you have the package?" he asked.

"No," said the man.

Leo's face twitched. "Well what the fuck? I thought you were going to be making the drop here. That's what my source told me on the phone."

"You fucked up the other day." The man jabbed Leo's chest with a finger. "It's not safe. We can't give you the package here."

This was the first time I'd ever heard the word "we" from an operative. I had that crawly feeling again. The man's eyes darted around the park as he talked to us. I followed his gaze. Nothing seemed to be wrong; the bums and Bostonians, the pigeons and the traffic were all doing exactly what they always did.

"So why are we even here?" Leo's eyes widened.

"I am here to give you information and information only," he said. "The phones are being watched too closely. There is a park in Malden. You have to meet us there tomorrow morning."

"Malden?" Leo looked as if he were going to flip out. "That's not even in Boston."

The raggedy man pulled out a slip of paper and threw it at me. "That's the address. Be there at 9 a.m. tomorrow morning at the top of the hill. And then we'll give you the package."

He got up and bolted into the subway station, leaving his roll of paper behind. My first instinct was to dart after him, but my ankle hurt too much.

"Malden," said Leo. "Whatever they are giving us must be really important."

"I guess." I just wanted to get out of there. "Let's go."

I kicked at the roll of paper. A half-eaten sandwich fell out. I wished I could see Danny again. I began to make my way toward the subway station. Leo's iPhone rang. He answered it, said a few words, and then gestured for me to stop. He looked nauseous. I looked away. I didn't want any more bad news. Holiday lights winked on and off on the other side of the street. Tinsel climbed streetlights. It was 3:30 p.m. and it was starting to get dark. Heavy gray clouds were moving in on one side of the Common. For the first time this season, it was beginning to look like Christmas. A family waddled past, the kids all bundled up in red and green. I'd been out all day and we'd accomplished nothing.

Leo slipped the phone into his pocket.

"I think you had better meet me at the bar tonight," he said in an uncharacteristically normal tone of voice. "My contact just called. He said that he has additional information for me. He's meeting me at eight. You should be there too."

I watched my breath steam in front of me in the cold air. The idea of spending another several hours sitting across from Leo in that awful bar made me tired.

"I was hoping to be home by now." I watched the family as they moved down the Common. "Maybe take the Fung-Wah tonight. I really thought we'd have this wrapped up by now."

"You couldn't leave anyway." Leo's eye twitched again.

I was sick of being told what I could and could not do. "Why the hell not?"

Leo gave me an odd look. "There's a blizzard tonight. The roads will be a mess." He shuddered, suddenly and violently. "Look, I have to go. I'll see you." He turned and walked away. I watched him as he went, jaywalking, his long greasy hair tucked into the collar of his leather jacket, slouching away toward Chinatown, his orange sneakers flashing in and out of view as he walked through a sea of people wearing black and brown boots.

I couldn't think of anywhere else to go, so I decided to take my chances and head back to the safehouse. Maybe put my feet up, take a nap. It took me an hour to get there. The apartment was dim when I let myself in. Slashes of steel-colored sky were visible through the closed blinds. I'd grabbed a yogurt and a plastic spoon from the corner store by way of dinner, and I sank onto the couch to eat it. The broken spring in the seat jabbed me intimately, and I cursed as loudly as I could, because, at that moment, swearing at a couch spring in an empty room was almost as satisfying as swearing at the Resistance.

"Watch your mouth," a muffled voice in the bathroom said. I jumped to my feet, splashing yogurt on myself. I did a quick survey of the room, scanning it for anything that I could use as a weapon, but the only thing handy was the plastic spoon. *What the hell,* I thought. *If the CIA can kill someone with a newspaper, I can kill someone with a plastic spoon in the dark, despite a complete lack of surprise.*

The toilet flushed, I heard water running in the sink and the bathroom door was pulled open from the inside. I tensed for my attack, raising the yogurt-smeared spoon in front of me. The bathroom door opened, and there was Danny.

"Sweetheart, what the hell are you doing?" he asked.

"I was having yogurt," I sank down on the couch casually, aiming just to the left of the broken spring. I was embarrassed to be so happy to see him. "What are you still doing here? Aren't you supposed to be at work?"

Danny smiled and shrugged. "I slept through it. They don't need me today anyways. So I thought I'd wait for you, since *someone* still hasn't given me her number. Where you been, angel?"

"Working," I replied and stuck a big spoonful of yogurt in my mouth.

Danny looked at me from the door of the bathroom.

"Yeah, how'd that go?"

Mouth full, I made an eh-well-you-know-work-is-work kind of facial expression.

Half of Danny's big mouth hitched upwards in a smile. "Yeah? Something wrong at work?"

"Well, one of the guys in our Boston office is sort of a moron." I shoveled more yogurt into my face and swallowed. "And whenever I come up here, we always end up having to work together, and he screws things up and then we both look bad, that sort of thing."

My phone vibrated. I looked down at it. An unidentified number.

"What's that, sweetheart?" Danny walked over.

My insides felt like they were buzzing. I read the message: New Orders: Get to Chinatown Bar at six.

"Hang on just a sec." I grinned up at him. "Work."

"Last night was great." He dropped a kiss on my head. "I'd love to buy you dinner."

I smiled and turned the phone into my shirt so he couldn't see the touchscreen or the fact that my hands were shaking. "Last night *was* great. Gimme a minute."

I texted quickly, holding the phone close to my chest: ALREADY ON IT. WHO IS THIS?

Danny dropped onto the couch, aiming for the other side of the spring. He reached a huge hand toward my lap and attempted to pull my legs onto his lap. "How's that ankle, angel? Can I rub your feet or something?"

I pulled back my legs, smiling like a crazy person. "Watch the spring."

The phone buzzed again. I looked down. My whole spine locked up when I read the text: BRING THE GIFT WE DROPPED FOR YOU LAST NIGHT NEAR CITY HALL. IT IS FOR LEO. THEN AWAIT FURTHER INSTRUCTIONS.

"Everything okay, angel?" Danny was watching me intently.

I did my best to keep my face cheerful. "Yeah," I chirped. "Everything is great. Is there anything in the fridge? I am starving."

"You're shaking." Danny's leaned back on the couch, and, for the first time, I registered what a big guy he was. The couch groaned under his weight. His legs stuck out so far that they blocked the way out of the room. He reached a massive arm toward me. I leaped up and saw stars.

"Low blood sugar. I told you that I was hungry." I slipped my phone into my pocket. It was buzzing.

"Aren't you going to get that?" Danny watched my phone disappear into my pants.

"They can wait. Let's get some dinner or something." I tried to breathe deeply and ignore the pain. My phone buzzed again.

"Sure." He was staring at me, his eyes cool over that warm smile. "What about Chinatown? You like Chinatown, don't you?"

"Sure. Great idea. Why not." I smiled, pulling my lips back from my teeth. My ribs felt like they were turning to ice. "Sounds great. Just let me just run into the other room and grab my bag."

"Your bag's right here." Danny picked it up off the floor.

I snatched it and stepped over his outstretched legs. "Of course it is. Let me just go to the bathroom."

I brought the bag in with me and pulled out my phone. Two texts, each reading PLEASE CONFIRM ORDERS.

I could hear Danny out in the apartment, moving around, humming to himself. I sat on the toilet and leaned my head against the cool tile wall. I knew what would happen if I didn't kill Leo. There were all kinds of stories floating around about the things that could get you disappeared by the Resistance. It seems like I heard a new one whenever I went on a run. My contact in Delaware told me about an assassin who'd refused to kill his mark. It's like that movie series where death can't be cheated. You don't know where they'll get you, and you don't know when they'll get you, but they will get you. You're already dead. They're just letting you walk around for a while. I probably wouldn't even get out of Boston.

"Sweetheart, what's taking you so long?" Danny's voice was right on the other side of the door. If someone came for me, and Danny was with me, they'd get him too.

ORDERS CONFIRMED, I texted. WILL ARRIVE WITH GIFT FOR LEO.

It was bitterly cold in the street. I slipped my hand into my messenger bag and touched the Glock. It was still warm, and I wrapped my chilly fingers around it as I followed Danny up the block toward Chinatown. The lyrics of "Happiness is a Warm Gun" floated into my brain and wouldn't leave. I found myself singing under my breath about going down, and about needing a fix.

Poor Leo. He was probably getting his fix right now. Last one he would ever get. My ankle throbbed.

The weather changed as we crossed over the Pike. A snow like granulated glass spun hard out of the great steel wool clouds, lacerating my cheeks. Danny was laughing and talking the whole time, but I didn't hear him; I hobbled along and thought that I deserved to be stung by anything that fell from heaven. The flakes swept around us in a fine, icy mist, hiding the rest of the world. The only reason I knew where we were going was because I was following Danny's loud, one-sided conversation.

"Coming down pretty good now, right sweetheart?" his voice shouted from somewhere right in front of me. "I can hardly see you back there. You know, we should go into the first restaurant we can that has big windows — it would really be something to be drinking hot tea while the blizzard comes down."

I drifted along unhappily in his wake. The idea of sharing a meal with Danny as if nothing were wrong and then excusing myself, and popping across the street to shoot my partner at eight gave me a feeling like spiders in my throat. But if I didn't, well, even inmates on death row get a last meal, I thought, and one dry sob rattled in my throat before I snapped my mouth shut on it.

I tried to concentrate on Leo, and tried to imagine putting the Glock to his head and squeezing the trigger. The image wouldn't come. Instead, I pictured him crying, pleading, I pictured him talking me out of it, and then I imagined taking a bullet in the back of the head when I agreed not to kill him. I imagined Danny, sitting across the street in a restaurant, maybe taking one in the forehead while he waited me to come back from the ladies room.

I couldn't stop singing that stupid song. The imaginary Beatles caroled in my brain about firearms and Mother Superior and about happiness, whatever that is.

By the time we finally set foot on the frozen swill that covered the gutters of Chinatown, I knew there was no way I would be able to sit through dinner. I had to get it over with, even if he wasn't there, and it meant waiting in that bar for hours until Leo wandered in, shaking with cold and fear. I needed time to clear my head, to really think and figure out what I was going to do when I saw him.

Danny's voice was getting further and further ahead of me in the falling snow. Without thinking too much about it, I had been struggling to keep up, but as I lost him for that second, it occurred to me that the answer to my problems had been coming down in drifts around me. I stopped and stood quietly, waiting for him to stride out of my life. Soon the other city noises swelled over his Boston accent, and he was lost in the Chinatown snow. I raised my head. For a moment, the world didn't feel so threatening. Everything seemed to be covered in powdered sugar, and I knew then that I could not spatter a white world like that with red.

It took me a few wrong turns to find it in the blizzard, but eventually I located the doorway to our bar. I pushed through the swirling snow toward it, knocking aside a pedestrian in my haste. The door was stuck. I gave it another push and it gave, grating over a drift of ice salt and snow that lay in a pile on the mat.

"Beware the goddamned hawk," I yelled, peering snowblind into the darkness. "Leo, I may kill you someday but not today. Let's get the hell out of here."

The bar was dark, empty and quiet. It smelled funny. I took a step forward, and felt a clunk underfoot. In a small puddle of melted snow lay the chimes that normally hung from the bar's door handle. I picked them up and hung them back on the door, clinking them together as I did so, but no heads appeared from the back room. The ancient bartender didn't appear, so I went to our customary booth and sat down.

My good leg jogged under the table. I don't know what I thought I was going to do once Leo appeared. I guess I thought that I'd grab him and we'd disappear into the storm with no plans, on the run, start Resistance-free lives somewhere.

Snow was piling up against the bar's one reinforced window. I wondered if Leo was upstairs in the opium den. *That must be where everyone is*, I thought. I picked up my phone.

AT SNOWFLOWER. WHERE ARE YOU?

Something buzzed, somewhere in the room. It sounded like my phone. I stood up. There was no one around. I looked down at my own phone. No missed texts. I picked it up again.

LEO? IF YOU'RE IN THE DEN I'M NOT COMING UP FOR YOU. Send.

More muffled buzzing. That did sound like one of the Resistance iPhones. Sounded like it was coming from behind the bar. Leo must have left his phone here, and the bartender stuck it behind the bar. I made my way to the bar.

DID YOU LEAVE YOUR PHONE IN THE BAR? BAD SECRET AGENT. winky emoticon. Send.

I leaned over the bar when I heard the muffled buzz. Leo was lying facedown in a dark pool. Someone else was back there, with him. Someone who smelled ripe. Bird guy. I didn't get a good look at them, just had time to register the hair and the jacket and his stupid, dirty, orange Converse sneakers before my own phone began making a very loud noise I had never heard before. I looked down. The touchscreen was doing something I'd never seen before, flashing red and white. And then there was a loud cracking noise and a rush of cold air. I looked up from my phone, which would not shut up, to see an indistinct figure standing in the open door, framed against the blizzard outside. He raised his arm toward me.

I hurled myself out of the way and fell behind a row of booths before the shooting even began, scrambling behind the furniture on the floor. He had to be snowblind, but that wouldn't help me. I realized, as soon as the gunfire stopped, that my iPhone was still screeching and flashing. I smashed the phone against the floor. For a second, it was quiet.

I crawled as far away as I could quietly, then peeked out from under a table. The gunman, back to me now, was looking at a phone of his own. He pressed a few buttons and my phone started screaming and flashing again. He opened fire in its direction.

Figures. My goddamned free iPhone *would* be a homing beacon. I reached into my messenger bag and pulled out the Glock. It seemed easy enough — I'd looked at it last night when Danny was sleeping. Plastic safety switch on the side, like a toy. I snapped it to the off position and stood up. I was going to have to do this fast. I needed the element of surprise, because in any shoot-out, I'd lose. I raised it in front of me.

The guy stopped firing and listened, staring at the place where my phone was carrying on. I squeezed the trigger. It felt funny. It gave a little, but nothing happened. I squeezed harder. The shot felt like an explosion at the end of my arm. The force of the bullet getting pushed out of the gun made my hand jump up and back, and I blinked, hard.

I didn't miss. I was pretty close to the guy. I don't know where I hit him, but he went down. He was alive, because shooting someone in real life is not like shooting them in the movies. It's not bang, you're dead. It's bang, you bleed.

I watched him writhe on the floor. My phone was still screaming and flashing. Then I took off, running out of the bar, pounding down the streets in the blizzard. I didn't even feel my ankle. Adrenaline is better than Vicodin. I don't remember much, just heading for South Station, to see if the Fung-Wah bus was running back to New York in the blizzard. Fung-Wah is crazy. There was a good chance of this happening. I still had my ticket in my pocket. I entered South Station running, slipped on the wet floor and fell on my face. Something in my foot cracked. I heard it at the same time my foot began to burn with a white-hot pain. I heard someone gasp.

"Are you okay, miss?" I didn't look at the guy who said it. If I stopped before I got where I was going, I thought I might be sick. Leo was dead. I'd maybe killed a guy. Some people were going to want to kill me. I didn't know where I was going after I got off the bus in New York. I had this fantasy of slipping into the city and just losing myself in all that humanity.

I scrambled to my feet and raced for the bus terminal. My foot wasn't working properly, but it didn't matter. I had a gun. I was going to make it home. I took the escalator two steps at a time. There was a Fung-Wah boarding. Those crazy bastards were actually sending a bus down to New York in this weather. I almost cheered. I lurched toward the bus terminal with my ticket in my fist.

A man stepped in front of me. He was built like a block.

"Out of my way, dude," I yelled, trying to slide around him and through the door that would take me to the platform.

"Freeze." The voice was behind me. I couldn't believe it. I tried to spin around.

"*Freeze.*"

The few people who were in the terminal were staring, muttering to each other.

I froze.

"Hands up. Drop that bag."

I did as I was told. Another man darted forward to grab my messenger bag. He rooted around in it and looked up at the person behind me.

"She's got a gun, detective."

The crowd gasped, right on cue.

"Turn around, slowly," said the voice behind me.

I breathed deeply and rotated on the foot that was still behaving. Danny was standing on the wet tiles, pointing a gun at my chest. No uniform, just a badge and a gun. He'd made it into the Academy after all.

Our eyes met over the gun, and I was sorry, so sorry. Sorry for the situation, sorry that he was the one who had to arrest me, sorry I was what I was. I was so fucking sorry, and he looked sorry too. But I was also damned if either one of us was going to say it aloud.

"Oh Danny," I whispered, "congratulations. You made the force."

His mouth twitched. "You have the right to remain silent" was what he said.

That's my story. My sister came to the lock-up to see me. *That* was a shit show. Wow. All upset about the publicity and her reputation or whatever. I guess my mom is all freaked out, too. My hair is growing out, so I look a lot like my sister and my mom. They're afraid people are going to see me on the cover of *The New York Post* and make the connection. Yeah. Not my problem. I dismissed the attorney the family tried to buy for me. He wouldn't be able to get me off anyway. Can you picture one of their hoity-toity lawyers trying to fight terrorism charges? Yeah. Me neither.

Guess that's not so much of a problem now.

You know, I was sort of looking forward to the trial. I was kind of hoping I'd finally find out what the Resistance is.

Do you know? It's not like I'm going to get a chance to tell anyone, right? I recognize that iPhone. I know why you're here.

About the Author

A.J. O'Connell is an author, journalist and adjunct professor who lives and labors in Connecticut. She holds an MFA in Creative Writing from Fairfield University. Her work has appeared on the website for National Public Radio, in *Citizen Culture Magazine*, *The Battered Suitcase*, *The Wheel* and various anthologies. She has reported for *The Norwalk Hour* and the *Boston Herald*.

11840045R10027

Made in the USA
Charleston, SC
24 March 2012